CW00811204

The *Unique*
SINGING
BOWL

Published by Binkey Kok Publications – Havelte/Holland

The *Unique* **SINGING** **BOWL**

Text Dick de Ruiter
Editing Valerie Cooper
Photography a.o. Eelco Boeijinga, Jaap Koning
Layout and cover design Jaap Koning
Printed and bound in the Netherlands

Published by Binkey Kok Publications
Hofstede De Weide Hoek – Havelte/Holland
Fax 00.31.521591925
E-mail binkey@inn.nl
ISBN 90-74597-46-7
© 2001 Binkey Kok Publications

CONTENTS

1 – ORIGINS

Many people are familiar with the sounds of the singing bowl, but others may have various questions about them. This brief introduction offers some background information and explains certain basic principles.

The original metal singing bowls come from the Far East. Although there is still a haze of secrecy hanging around the question of the origins and original use of the bowls, we do know that in the very distant past they were used in sound rituals and ceremonies. It was only in the second half of the last century, when China invaded Tibet in the 1950s, that the first singing bowls came from the Himalayas to the West. At first, it was suggested that they were mere offering bowls for holding special substances during Tibetan monastic rituals, until it was discovered that they produce a hauntingly beau-

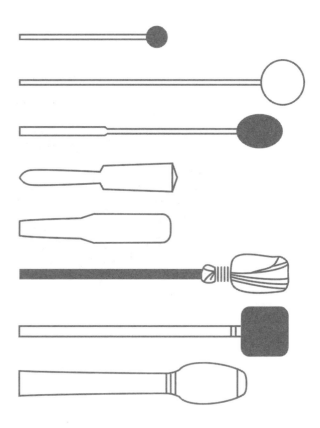

tiful and pure sound, containing many harmonic overtones. Their special alloy—usually consisting of seven different metals, the original conception of which remains a mystery to us—determines the timbre and the duration of the sound of the bowls.

In addition to the Tibetan singing bowls that originated in the Himalayas, there are also Japanese and Thai varieties, and each kind has its own characteristic sound, shape, and use. Yet, the Tibetan bowls remain the purest in sound and overtones. The incredible craftsmanship of the old masters who, centuries ago, were able to manufacture these works of art with their mysterious power and sound, deserves immense respect and further study. The original, authentic bowls haven't been made for about fifty years. The purity of modern, cast specimens falls far short of that of the ancient bowls. At present, 80-90 percent of the bowls on the market are fake! Of course, for the layman, it is difficult to check a bowl's true origin.

There are also crystal singing bowls, which are cast in the USA from quartz. They look brilliant and have a very specific sound, that can be tuned exactly to a certain tone. Crystal, however, is a pure conductor of sound (consider the crystal radio receiver). There has been insufficient research of the effects or possible dangers of crystal bowl sound transmissions upon the body's physical functions.

It is highly recommended to place some pieces of rock crystal between the singing bowls. The rock crystal will purify and enhance the interaction between the bowls, while the resonance of the bowls purifies the crystals.

2 – THE METAL ELEMENT

In the ancient Far Eastern teachings of the five elements, which are as old as living memory extends, the metal element stands for clarity and purity. As a medium, its function is to link earth, water, wood and fire. After all, to free metal, which is hidden inside the earth, you need wood and fire. In Feng Shui, the ancient teachings of harmony, the following properties are given to metal—purification, contraction, connection with water.

The metal alloy of a singing bowl determines—together with the shape—its characteristic timbre. Like all other things natural that make sound, a singing bowl also has a whole range of under- and overtones. The purity of these tones is revealed if a singing bowl has been shaped the right way, and when it is used for therapy. It is this purity—mostly of the overtones—by which one can recognize the handmade quality and authenticity of the bowl. Antique singing bowls may occasionally sound out of tune; this impurity is in most cases caused by damage or alteration of the original bowl due to dents and deformations.

Fine-tuning is done by making grooves just below the edge of the singing bowl. Although this fine-tuning is meant to produce as pure a vibration as possible, true to its vibrational figure (Yantra), the sound can sound dishar-

monic—at least to the Western ear. However, Eastern sound tradition recognizes five sub-tones between each of the seven primary tones.

Most ancient bowls are shaped from an alloy—a melted mix of several metals, such as gold, silver, lead, mercury, copper, tin, and iron. It has been said that the best singing bowls contain meteorite instead of iron. However, the proportions of the various different metals, together with the shape of the bowl, determine its final timbre and effects. Just as the purity of the crystal determines how fine a wineglass will "sing," so does the amount of precious metals determine the purity and clarity of the basic tone and overtones in the singing bowl, as well as the duration of the sound. A good singing bowl should resonate for a very long time after striking, and the sound dies gradually, not suddenly.

3 – THE SHAPE OF THE SINGING BOWL

I t is evident that a singing bowl's size determines the sound and pitch that it generates, but its design is a co-factor; for instance, the height of the edge, the thickness of the metal, the difference between base and sides, and the molding of the base.

Most Himalayan singing bowls currently in use have a characteristic design (see picture) with the edge (thickness, line, decoration), and the angle of the side in relation to the bottom, as significant features. A good singing bowl is never misshapen; the curves must be harmonious. While playing a singing bowl, the performer usually places the bowl on a ring of cloth, or rests it in his or her hand. If the base of the bowl is rather flat, it will not resonate well while resting on a flat surface.

The thickness of the material—and, as previously mentioned, the composition of the alloy—determines the ultimate range of overtones that the bowl is able to produce.

Authentic bowls show clearly how the maker has shaped the mould; there are little flat spots visible all over the surface. These have to harmonically follow the shape, otherwise there is a dissonance in the overtones.

As the thickness of the bowl increases, so does the audibility of the undertones; the thinner this layer is—and the smaller the bowl—the more the overtones can be audibly discerned.

When the bowl is struck there should be no secondary sounds, such as rattling. In authentic, well-shaped bowls the sound remains pure.

• Further reading:
E.R. Jansen, Singing Bowls – A Practical Handbook for Instruction and Use. Binkey Kok Publications, Havelte/Holland 1992 / *Outer characteristics*

4 – VIBRATION / The Transference of Sound-Resonance

re-sonare / re-verberate

N *ada brahma—the world is sound.* The ancient Indians knew this, and modern science confirms it: everything is vibrating, even the most solid matter.

Our bodies consist mostly of water, and water is easily reverberated; a stone cast in water causes vibrations that continue evenly both over the surface and underneath it. External vibrations meet with a wide response in our bodies and have great influence, not only through our ears, but mainly through the resonance of our cellular structures, whether the source of vibration is light, electromagnetism, or sound. Our bodies therefore are capable of orienting to sound and vibration. The sound and vibration of singing bowls is regulatory and harmonizing.

In our modern Western society, the world around us provides many vibrations that have a negative influence: trafficnoise, high-voltage cables, fluorescent lighting. The effect is chaotic and draining for our body/mind system.

The harmonic sounds of the bowls can provide a counterbalance here.

Because the multi-harmonic sounds ('harmonics') are so perfectly tuned, and because the vibration works harmonically, we can create order again in this chaos of negative vibrations. We just have to sit or lay down, relax and open up; the rest will happen by itself.

We call this a *sound-bath* or *sound-massage*. We can make this process as harmonious as possible by using soft (full spectrum) light (or tempered sunlight), minimizing disturbances from outside, maintaining a pleasant temperature, and by working with colors and shapes (Feng Shui), etc. But in the sound-bath the most important factor is that the sound source (i.e. singing bowls or very good speakers) is of a high, pure quality. This means the volume should be high enough to make our bodies vibrate, but not so loud that it is unpleasant for the ears; and the basic, under- and overtones of the singing bowls should be perfectly harmonic. Daily 15 (minimum) to 60 (maximum) minutes of such a sound-bath can perform miracles on our whole being, physically and mentally.

In order to consciously experience and creatively interact with a sound-bath, one is advised to sit down about 10 feet (3 meters) from the speakers, which are preferably placed on the floor.

To use a sound-bath as pure relaxation, lay down, with bare feet toward the speakers. Of course, it works best when real, live singing bowls are being

used, directly on and around the body. In that case, there is a very real sound massage, because the vibration is un-encoded and complete, resulting in optimal harmonization of our body cells.

However, with good speakers (preferably at least 50-watt surround sound), excellent results can be expected.

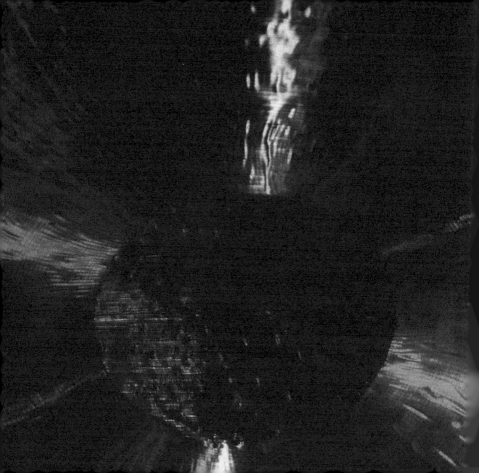

5 – ENERGY CHARGING / RELAXATION

I t is evident that some sounds build up energy, while others have a relaxing influence. Relaxing means neither stimulating, nor draining. Most sounds around us, such as street noise, the fridge, fluorescent lighting, air conditioning, and so on, are debilitating; they tire us and, moreover, they disturb the fine balance within both our physical and mental lives.

Because good singing bowls always work as harmonizers, we simply have to make a choice between either energy-enhancing or energy-easing sounds. Because of the wide choice in available recordings there are ample possibilities. Volume plays a crucial role here, together with the quality and capacity of the loudspeakers! The sound may be very relaxing in terms of structure and continuity, but if the volume is too loud, such a sound would be stimulating. So if we wish to relax, the volume must always be pleasantly soft; literally a caress for ear and body.

To experience the energetic effects at their best, the surrounding conditions must also be considered: comfortable temperature, stillness, comfortable lighting, and also the best posture (refer back to section 4, regarding the *sound-bath*).

It is, of course, advisable to first acquaint yourself with the recordings in

order to choose a suitable program from the various tracks.

Later, you can simply choose *intuitively* which part and which performance are best suited for a certain situation.

For a relaxing effect, lying down is the optimal posture; for a stimulating effect the straight sitting position or even standing up is preferable.

• For further studies we refer to *Steven Halpern's* book Tuning the Human Instrument (HarperSanFrancisco, 1985).

6 – STRIKING AND RUBBING

T he techniques most frequently used in playing the Himalayan singing bowls are striking them or stroking/rubbing the edge firmly, yet gently ("sounding"). To this end, various sorts of striking or rubbing sticks can be used. There are smooth, wooden rubbing sticks, as well as sticks in various other sizes and materials, sometimes with a rubber strip around the base. You can also find small hardwood or metal strikers, and large felt hammers.

The particular significance of the rubbing method is that it is capable of producing a variety of tones, undertones and overtones, depending upon the position of the rubbing stick and the rubbing tempo. While gently circling the bowl, the stick produces an almost continuous keynote that can be varied in intensity by turning a little faster or more slowly. Sometimes the bowl is struck first in order to produce the basic tone. By rubbing the stick around the edge of the bowl this tone is perpetuated, and the other tones are allowed to generate. Preferably, however, one makes the bowl sing without striking it first, so that, as it were, the sound gradually evolves from the bowl as opposed to being "knocked" out of it.

It is just as possible to use a violin bow to sound a singing bowl.

Sometimes the performer even fills the bowl partly with water, which at a certain intensity of sound will start spattering: hence, the humorous name of 'splashing bowls.' The water naturally makes a difference to the sound of the bowl as well.

By varying the angle of the stick or the pressure on the edge of the bowl, new tones are created: under- and overtones; sometimes separately, sometimes simultane-

ously, weaving themselves into a web of sound. Angled at the edge, or parallel to the side, each technique produces its own unique sound spectrum. This means that from just one bowl it is possible to audibly originate a range of 5 or 6 under- and/or overtones. The player can even accentuate one particular tone, so that the others diminish or sound softer.

Naturally, using more bowls, both large and small, an integral sound tapestry can be created, in which the under- and overtones can co-exist and supplement each other, creating in turn a completely new sound experience

A metal or hardwood striker produces a sharp, clear tone from the bowl.

A felt striker obviously gives a much softer, friendlier response.

Finally, some artists use their mouths near the edge of the bowl to accentuate certain overtones—truly exceptional!

Although it's up for debate, some therapists maintain that there is an effective difference between rotating a rubbing stick clockwise and counterclockwise on the edge of the bowl.

O

7 – THE UNIQUE SINGING BOWL

The sound of a singing bowl can be compared to no other musical instrument. This is but one reason why the singing bowl is so unique.

It is only during the last decade of the 20th century that the versatility and predominantly therapeutic effect of the bowls has been discovered and researched

We now have gifted sound therapists who, by means of treatment with singing bowls, are able to instill deeper levels of harmony and energy into our lives. The possession of just a single, carefully selected singing bowl can work miracles in the hands of a gifted player.

Resonance plays an important role here. These external vibrations harmonize sympathetically with our original internal frequencies. A calming effect follows, and further influences the brainwaves, reducing them to a quieter vibrational level. Comparable results cannot be found in any other therapeutic musical instrument.

A bowl either suits you or not. This is a question of intensive 'testing'—listen, feel and experience thoroughly. If you feel nothing at all, or the bowl

simply does not sound pleasant at that moment, this usually means it is not going to work for you. Look further; don't settle with 'almost' and don't let yourself be talked into anything you don't want, otherwise you will buy a story instead of a bowl. If you feel comfortable, in whatever way—more relaxed or more clear in the head—then the singing bowl has touched upon a tender string within you.

This test is obviously just as valid for the various parts of a singing bowl recording; you can also choose and feel, dependent upon your present mood, what the sound does to you at that particular moment.

8 – THE HANDS OF THE MUSICIAN

A musical piece stands or falls with the quality of its performance. Thus, a master can fail on a bad instrument, just as an inadequate artist can ruin a good one.

Assuming the singing bowl has a pure sound, it is left to the hands of the musician to determine how this sound will ring and the effects it will have.

On this CD you will discover many masterpieces. An open listener will be able to experience the energy of the artist generated through the soundplay.

No instrument can render the mental state of the player as well as a singing bowl. A touch should be subtle, a tone pure—it cannot be otherwise—the musician bares his or her soul before the public. Performing on one or more singing bowls is to reveal oneself; a revelation in gossamer soundplay...

S inging bowls are a divine exception in a world of music and sound. Although their origins remain hidden in the mists of time, we can all gratefully make use of the wonderful colors and shapes these sounds create. Their liberating effect upon rigid mental structures, their attunement with the body's own vibrational makeup, and their harmonizing influence upon our whole being instilles a feeling of wonder.

The recordings presented here are, piece for piece, small miracles of healing sound.

Put it to the test: treat yourself for a week with a daily sound-bath, and feel the difference!

O

SAMPLE RECORDINGS
OF SINGING BOWLS ON THIS ALBUM:

Track 1   SINGING BOWL MEDITATION
           by Hans de Back – track 1 – 5:00
Track 2   SINGING BOWL MEDITATION
           by Hans de Back – track 2 – 5:00
Track 3   CHAKRA MEDITATION
           by Hans de Back – track 3 – 5:00
Track 4   CHAKRA MEDITATION
           by Hans de Back – track 7 – 5:00
Track 5   SHABDA
           by Rainer Tillmann – track 2 – 5:00
Track 6   SHABDA
           by Rainer Tillmann – track 6 – 5:00
Track 7   NADA 1
           by Rainer Tillmann – track 1 – 5:00
Track 8   NADA 1
           by Rainer Tillmann – track 3 – 5:00

Tracks 1-2:

SINGING BOWL MEDITATION

Healing sounds of various bowls, bells, and gongs, finely tuned to one another for a simple but awe-inspiring interplay ranging from the very deep reverberation of the gongs to the high pitch of the temple bells.

Tracks 3-4:

CHAKRA MEDITATION

This recording contains seven selected improvizations on Asian gongs and bells, and can be used as a tool for exploration of the seven energy centers in the human body. The performer has not applied the usual concept of basic tones for each chakra, but uses the deep resonance of the complex harmonic overtones, creating an atmosphere of contemplation.

Tracks 5-6:

SHABDA – THE PURITY OF SOUND

If you want a continuous tapestry of sound, highly conducive for meditative practice, this recording is the perfect choice. The eight parts contain naturally occurring sound wave frequencies to relax brain activity. Incredible sound quality.

Tracks 7-8:
NADA 1 – THE SOUNDS OF PLANETS II

This recording contains the pure, meditative sounds of singing bowls, bells and cymbals, which correlate to the planetary ratio harmonics, according to scientists like Hans Cousto. There are four themes: *Year Tone, Saturn, Venus,* and *Sun.*

Tracks 9-10:
NADA 2 – THE SOUNDS OF PLANETS II

Follow-up to the same breathtaking sound constellations of the other planets in our solar system. The themes are: *Moon, Neptune/Pluto, Jupiter, Uranus, Mars,* and *Mercury.*

Tracks 11-12:
DEVA – CRYSTAL SOUNDS
Music for the Nature Devas

This CD is comprised exclusively of crystal singing bowls, accompanied by bells, gongs, chimes, and cymbals. The very special, mysterious sound of the crystal bowls is incomparable to any other musical instrument.

Tracks 13-14:

SOMA – SOUNDS FOR HEALING I

A most exceptional combination of ancient metal bowls with contemporary crystal singing bowls. The first track features this partnership; as does the second, in combination with other instruments, such as cymbals and chimes. Includes soothing 3-D effects that create a relaxed, meditative, imaginary realm.

Tracks 15-16:

PRANA – SOUNDS FOR HEALING 2

For your living energy

The extraordinary art of playing large flat gongs and singing bowls is mastered by *Rainer Tillmann*. Using original, impressive instruments and superb recording equipment, the result is fascinating: every track is a sound surprise you can use to recharge your energy or for meditative purposes.

Rainer Tillmann

Hans de Back

Look for the full-length CDs sampled here at your local book or music store.
If your store doesn't stock them, or can't order them for you, you can order
them directly from Samuel Weiser, Inc.,
P.O. Box 612, York Beach, ME 03910-0612, toll free: 1-800-423-7087.

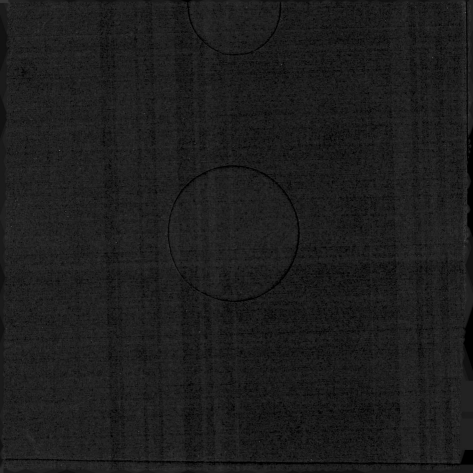